Ghosts Don't Ride Wild Horses

by Debbie Dadey
and
Marcia Thornton Jones

illustrated by John Steven Gurney

SCHOLASTIC INC.
New York Toronto London Auckland Sydney
Mexico City New Delhi Hong Kong

For Coco-Mo, a new furry friend,
and in memory of two special
four-legged friends, Tazz and Purrl
—MTJ

To Marcia Jones with many thanks
and to Lee Phillips
—DD

ISBN 0-439-21584-6

12 11 10 9 8 7 6 5 4 3 2 1 2 3 4 5 6/0

Printed in the U.S.A. 40

First Scholastic printing, March 2001

Ghosts Don't Ride Wild Horses

There are more books about the Bailey School Kids!
Have you read these adventures?

#1 Vampires Don't Wear Polka Dots
#2 Werewolves Don't Go to Summer Camp
#3 Santa Claus Doesn't Mop Floors
#4 Leprechauns Don't Play Basketball
#5 Ghosts Don't Eat Potato Chips
#6 Frankenstein Doesn't Plant Petunias
#7 Aliens Don't Wear Braces
#8 Genies Don't Ride Bicycles
#9 Pirates Don't Wear Pink Sunglasses
#10 Witches Don't Do Backflips
#11 Skeletons Don't Play Tubas
#12 Cupid Doesn't Flip Hamburgers
#13 Gremlins Don't Chew Bubble Gum
#14 Monsters Don't Scuba Dive
#15 Zombies Don't Play Soccer
#16 Dracula Doesn't Drink Lemonade
#17 Elves Don't Wear Hard Hats
#18 Martians Don't Take Temperatures
#19 Gargoyles Don't Drive School Buses
#20 Wizards Don't Need Computers
#21 Mummies Don't Coach Softball
#22 Cyclops Doesn't Roller-Skate
#23 Angels Don't Know Karate
#24 Dragons Don't Cook Pizza
#25 Bigfoot Doesn't Square Dance
#26 Mermaids Don't Run Track
#27 Bogeymen Don't Play Football
#28 Unicorns Don't Give Sleigh Rides
#29 Knights Don't Teach Piano
#30 Hercules Doesn't Pull Teeth
#31 Ghouls Don't Scoop Ice Cream
#32 Phantoms Don't Drive Sports Cars
#33 Giants Don't Go Snowboarding
#34 Frankenstein Doesn't Slam Hockey Pucks
#35 Trolls Don't Ride Roller Coasters
#36 Wolfmen Don't Hula Dance
#37 Goblins Don't Play Video Games
#38 Ninjas Don't Bake Pumpkin Pies
#39 Dracula Doesn't Rock and Roll
#40 Sea Monsters Don't Ride Motorcycles
#41 The Bride of Frankenstein Doesn't Bake Cookies
#42 Robots Don't Catch Chicken Pox
#43 Vikings Don't Wear Wrestling Belts
The Bailey School Kids Joke Book
Super Special #1: Mrs. Jeepers Is Missing!
Super Special #2: Mrs. Jeepers' Batty Vacation
Super Special #3: Mrs. Jeepers' Secret Cave
Super Special #4: Mrs. Jeepers in Outer Space
Super Special #5: Mrs. Jeepers' Monster Class Trip

Contents

1

Hog-tied

"This might be the best field trip we've ever been on," Howie told his friends. He wore cowboy boots and jeans. "The Wild West was full of adventure and danger."

Liza wore a sunbonnet and shawl. "I don't need an adventure and I definitely don't want to be in any danger," she said.

Melody tipped her cowboy hat in Liza's direction. "Don't worry. This is just a pretend pioneer settlement."

Howie nodded at Melody's words. "There's absolutely nothing to worry about. In fact, I think it will be fun learning about gold miners, cattle rustling, and pioneer history firsthand."

Eddie was not interested in learning history. He wore sweatpants and an old T-shirt, but he did carry a long rope.

"Forget history," Eddie said. "Bring on the bucking broncos and charging bulls. I'll hog-tie everyone and throw them to the ground."

To prove his point, Eddie twirled his rope high over his head and tried to lasso Melody. The rope sailed over Melody and landed in the branches of the oak tree.

Melody grabbed the other end of the rope from Eddie. She wrapped it around him, pinning his arms down. "You better behave or Mrs. Jeepers will hog-tie YOU and leave you as wolf bait," she warned.

Liza shivered and pulled her shawl tighter as the sun disappeared behind a cloud. "Heading into the wilderness with a vampire teacher is not my idea of a good time," she said. "What if Mrs. Jeepers does leave us as a werewolf snack?"

The kids looked across the playground. Their teacher was organizing the rest of the third-graders near a big yellow school bus. Mrs. Jeepers was not a normal teacher. She came from Transyl-

vania and lived in a haunted house. Everybody was sure she was a vampire.

"Going *any* place with *any* teacher is a kid's worst nightmare," Eddie added. "Especially when we have to learn history!"

The bus's door opened. "It looks like it's time to go," Howie said as he pulled Eddie free from his rope. "Don't worry. This trip will be fun!"

"I hope you're right," Liza said, but she didn't sound too sure.

2

Pioneer Frontier

The four friends made their way across the playground and joined the other third-graders as they climbed aboard the bus. Mrs. Gurney, the driver, put the bus into gear. They rode half of the morning, leaving Bailey City far behind.

Finally, Mrs. Gurney turned down a dirt road. A wooden sign read PIONEER FRONTIER. After twenty minutes on a bumpy dirt road, the bus rolled to a stop.

"It looks like we've left the twenty-first century and landed smack-dab in the 1800s," Howie said as the kids looked out the window.

"Who wants to be in the 1800s?" Eddie asked. "They didn't even have TV then."

"Or indoor toilets," Melody added.

Liza looked worried, but Melody patted

Liza's arm. "I'm sure Pioneer Frontier has modern plumbing now."

The kids peered out the bus window at Pioneer Frontier. A dirt road ran down the center of a town full of weathered wooden buildings. A snack-bar saloon with swinging doors stood between a general store with dirty windows and a boardinghouse with hitching posts in front. At the far end of the road the kids saw a picnic shelter, a livery stable, and a corral. Behind the corral a sign pointed to the bunkhouses. Tumbleweeds rolled down the deserted road.

"This is eerie," Liza whispered.

"We're so far from civilization that a gang of bandits could raid our camp and nobody would ever know," Melody whispered.

"It looks exactly like a real live ghost town!" Howie added.

Liza gasped. "I don't want to spend the night in a ghost town with a vampire teacher!"

“Never fear, Eddie is here. I’ll lasso every vampire, bandit, and ghost,” Eddie said as he swung the rope over his head and tossed it in Howie’s direction.

Eddie missed Howie and instead his rope landed right on Carey’s head. Carey’s father ran Bailey City Bank. She usually got her own way. She also liked looking perfect. Carey glared at Eddie as she tried to smooth her curly blond hair.

Mrs. Jeepers flashed her green eyes at Eddie. Liza gulped when Mrs. Jeepers reached for her green brooch. Melody closed her eyes. Most kids believed Mrs. Jeepers’ pin was magic, but luckily for Eddie the bus door swung open and Mrs. Jeepers never got a chance to rub her brooch. A park ranger stepped on board to welcome the kids to the Pioneer Frontier.

Howie was the first to recognize the ranger from their day hike to Ruby Mountain, where they had learned about

natural habitats near Bailey City. "That's Ranger Lily," he whispered to his friends.

The kids had been sure Ranger Lily was hunting for Bigfoot while they hiked through the woods of Ruby Mountain. Ranger Lily was tall and thin with short dark hair, and she loved the outdoors.

Eddie wasn't so quiet. He hopped up on his seat and yelled over everybody's head, "Aren't you the same lady that was looking for the Bigfoot monster?"

A few kids giggled. Mrs. Jeepers' hand rested on her brooch. But Ranger Lily didn't look embarrassed at all. She smiled at Eddie and shrugged.

"There are people who spend their entire lives looking for something," Ranger Lily said. "In fact, some people spend more than one lifetime searching."

"How can that be?" Melody asked, but thundering hooves drowned out her words.

3

Mystery Cowboy

A herd of horses galloped past the bus, kicking a gray cloud of dust high into the air. Three cowboys and two cowgirls rode after them, driving the horses into the corral at the end of the street. The horses pawed the ground and a few reared up on their hind legs.

"Those horses look wilder than Eddie," Carey said.

Ranger Lily nodded. "They are wild. The surrounding hills are full of horses. Every year Pioneer Frontier rounds some up. If they didn't, there would be too many wild horses and the horses wouldn't have enough to eat."

"Where did the horses come from?" Liza asked.

Ranger Lily looked out a bus window

at the horses. "Passing pioneers left many things in these hills. Horses, pigs, and plants, to name a few," she explained. "But these hills are also full of secrets left by the pioneers."

"There's a horse trying to get away!" Liza interrupted and pointed out the window.

The kids looked up toward the top of a hill. The sun beat down and the heat made everything wavy, but the kids were

able to see a man dressed entirely in smoky gray, swinging a rope over his head. He flung the rope toward a horse the color of the clouds. The rope sailed through the air and landed around the wild horse's head.

The horse tossed its mane. It pawed the ground and backed away. Then it reared high into the air. Still, the cowboy in gray held tight to the rope, refusing to let go.

Ranger Lily gasped and wiped a clean spot on the smudged window to get a closer look.

"That cowboy sure is brave," Howie said.

"Or crazy," Liza whispered.

Eddie shrugged. "I could do that with one arm tied behind my back," he bragged. Eddie slung his rope across the aisle of the bus to prove his point. His rope landed on a suitcase in the storage bin over Carey's head. When Eddie tugged on his rope, the suitcase toppled into the aisle and popped open.

Underwear spilled everywhere. Carey shrieked and jumped out of her seat, hurrying to stuff her unmentionables back in her suitcase. The rest of the third-graders laughed so hard, they forgot all about the cowboy on the hill. "You'll pay for this," Carey told Eddie through clenched teeth.

"That cowboy is much better than Eddie when it comes to roping wild horses," Melody said with a giggle. "Who is he?"

Ranger Lily shook her head. "I haven't a clue," she said. "That cowboy is a total mystery."

4

Gold Fever

"This is for sissies," Eddie griped after the kids had stowed their sleeping bags and backpacks in the bunkhouses. All around the town costumed park leaders showed groups of kids about pioneer life.

One cluster of kids worked by the barn, churning butter. Another group stitched a quilt in the shade of a nearby cabin. A third group panned for gold near a stream that trickled down the hill-side. Melody, Howie, Liza, Eddie, and Carey kneaded bread dough with Ranger Lily under the picnic shelter.

Eddie pointed to the group near the water. "Why can't I be with them?" he complained. "Looking for gold is more exciting than mixing flour and water."

Ranger Lily glanced at the kids by the

stream. They knelt on the ground and swished water out of pans with wire bottoms, hoping to find big lumps of gold.

"That's exactly what miners thought during the gold rush," Ranger Lily told Eddie. "But they were wrong. Greed was the ruin of many men. All for a few shiny pieces of rock."

Suddenly, the wind whipped up. Carey and Liza scattered, trying to collect the bread recipes that blew off the picnic table. They froze when a howling noise echoed from the hills right behind the picnic shelter.

"What was that?" Liza asked, her voice trembling.

"It sounds like someone crying," Melody told her.

"Somebody," Ranger Lily said, "or something."

"I bet it's a coyote howling," Howie said.

Ranger Lily nodded. "Coyotes do live in these hills," she said. "They always have. In fact, there is a legend about a pioneer who loved the sound of the coyotes so much that he settled right here instead of moving farther west with the rest of his wagon train."

"What happened to him?" Eddie asked.

"Greed got to him, too," Ranger Lily said. "In fact, he caught the worst case of gold fever ever known in these hills. It led to his ruin."

"How?" Liza asked.

But Ranger Lily didn't answer. She walked to the edge of the picnic shelter where the sun shone bright and peered up into the woods, as if she expected to see something there. The leaves on the trees trembled and a flock of birds suddenly took flight. Three horses in the nearby corral reared and galloped to the far side of the enclosure. Ranger Lily's face turned pale. Droplets of sweat dotted her forehead.

"Are you all right?" Melody asked.

Ranger Lily wiped the sweat from her

forehead. "It must be the sun," she told Melody. "I thought I heard something."

"Maybe a cold drink of water would help," Liza suggested.

Ranger Lily shook her head, as if trying to shake spiderwebs from her hair. "That's exactly what I need," she said with a weak smile.

Without saying another word, Ranger Lily headed across the dusty road.

Eddie waited until she disappeared through the swinging doors of the snack-bar saloon. "Finally," he said, "time for a little fun."

"You'd better behave," Melody warned him. "Ranger Lily will be right back."

Eddie ignored Melody. He grabbed his bread dough and molded it into a dinosaur. Then he slung it across the table. It landed right on Carey's head.

Carey pulled the dough from her hair. Flour stuck to her springy blond curls. "I've had it with you. Just wait until

Ranger Lily hears about this," Carey said before stomping after their instructor.

"You've done it now," Howie said. "Carey is determined to get you in trouble."

"Not if I stop her first," Eddie huffed. He grabbed his lasso and swung it in the air, ready to drop it over Carey and hog-tie her to the picnic table. But before he could let it fly, a long, dark shadow fell over them all.

5

Coyote Pete

Eddie, Melody, Howie, and Liza turned to see a thin man standing in a beam of sunlight at the edge of the picnic shelter. The sun rose in waves from the shelter's concrete. The kids tried blocking out the sun with their hands to see who stood there. The stranger wore gray jeans, a gray shirt, and a gray cowboy hat. In fact, everything he wore was gray, even his cowboy boots with spurs. Deep wrinkles lined his face and he carried a rope.

When he spoke, his voice sounded like a rusty chain. "It looks like you need a little help a-swinging that itty-bitty string," he told Eddie.

Eddie stood up tall and puffed out his chest. "I don't need any help," he bragged.

"I'm the roughest, toughest cowpoke in these parts."

Melody giggled. "I'm not sure about being the roughest and toughest, but you sure are the orneriest kid in our third grade."

Eddie lifted his rope to lasso Melody. He swung it over his head, but it stopped dead in midair.

The man in gray had reached out and grabbed the rope. With a flick of his wrist he pulled it from Eddie's grasp.

"Give me back my rope," Eddie snapped.

The man dropped the rope at Eddie's feet. "You remind me of someone," the stranger said in a raspy voice. He pointed at Eddie's chest. "I go by the name of Coyote Pete. You ever heard that name before?"

Eddie reached down to pick up his rope. "I've never heard that name in my entire life," he said.

Coyote Pete squinted at Eddie as if he was trying to decide if Eddie was lying. Finally Coyote Pete nodded. "I've got my eye on you," he said to Eddie. "What's your name?"

Eddie opened his mouth to speak, but just then Ranger Lily and Carey pushed through the swinging doors of the snack-bar saloon. The old cowboy glanced their way before pointing a crooked finger at Eddie. "If you're who I think you might be, you're as good as rattlesnake meat. You can mark my words."

To prove his point, Coyote Pete took his rope and with a flick of his wrist he sent it sailing through the air. It landed around a bag of flour. Coyote Pete pulled the rope tight and squeezed the bag. Flour sprayed all over the picnic area, leaving the kids in a fog of white.

When the dust finally settled, the kids looked around. Flour covered everything under the picnic shelter, including the

FLOUR

kids. But Coyote Pete had disappeared without a trace.

Ranger Lily marched up to the shelter as the last of the flour settled. With her hands on her hips, she glared at Eddie.

"I told you Eddie was nothing but trouble," Carey said with a huff. "Look what he did! He ruined everything!"

Ranger Lily handed a broom to Eddie. "Get busy, buster," she said, leaving Eddie to clean up the mess.

"I'll get even with Carey if it's the last thing I do," Eddie said between clenched teeth as he attacked the flour with his broom. "Carey *and* Coyote Pete!"

6

Blackheart Eddie

That evening, the kids sat around a campfire roasting marshmallows. "Did you enjoy learning how to clean house?" Carey teased Eddie as she walked behind him.

Eddie tossed a marshmallow at Carey's back. "She drives me crazy," he mumbled.

"It wasn't all her fault," Howie told him. "Coyote Pete is the one that made the mess with his lariat."

Eddie rolled his eyes. "He used a rope, silly."

"A lariat is a rope you use to lasso things," Howie explained.

Melody nodded. "He sure was good with that lariat. I didn't think there was anybody who was that good. Not anymore."

"He must practice," Liza said. "After all, practice makes perfect."

"Then he's had years and years of practice," Melody said. "I wonder who taught him how to rope like that."

"I bet Ranger Lily knows," Liza said. She raised her hand high in the air.

"Do you know about Coyote Pete?" she asked.

Ranger Lily's eyes got big. She took off her hat, ran her fingers through her hair, and sat down hard on a nearby log. "Where did you hear that name?" she asked Liza. "I didn't mention it when I started to tell you the legend."

"What legend?" Melody asked.

"The legend of Coyote Pete," Ranger Lily told her.

"So you do know who he is!" Eddie blurted. "Tell us about him!"

Ranger Lily perched her hat on the back of her head before speaking. "You remember I told you about the pioneer who loved the sound of coyotes? Well, his

name was Coyote Pete. Pete was a cowpoke making his way west with a wagon train. But when they camped here, in this very spot, he fell in love with the sound of coyotes singing to the full moon. Instead of moving west with the rest of the pioneers, he settled right here. He was harmless enough, at first. But then," Ranger Lily said as she looked all the campers in the eye, "he caught the fever."

"I had a fever once," Carey said as she patted her hair. "It took the curl right out of my hair."

"It wasn't that kind of fever," Ranger Lily explained. "It was worse than any cold or flu. It was gold fever, and when somebody caught it there was no curing it until they had their hands on a bag of gold. Coyote Pete tried, but he wasn't lucky when it came to panning for gold. Somebody else was, though. A friend of his struck it rich right before Coyote Pete's eyes."

"Coyote Pete should've been happy for his friend," Liz said.

Ranger Lily shook her head. "He wasn't. Coyote Pete decided he had to get his hands on that gold — even if it was the last thing he did. He decided to do the worst thing a man could do. He planned to rob his friend. Of course, he never got his chance."

"Why not?" Eddie asked.

"Coyote Pete was stopped," Ranger Lily said. "Stopped by Blackheart Eddie."

"Blackheart Eddie?" Liza shrieked.

"That's a great name," Eddie said. "He sounds mean."

"But he wasn't," Ranger Lily said. "In fact, he was nothing more than a kid. Like you. He even had red hair and freckles. He got his name by playing silly tricks on people. He fooled people all the time because he was smart. Smarter than Coyote Pete himself. Blackheart Eddie figured out what Coyote Pete was up to and tricked him into admitting his plan to the sheriff. After that, Coyote Pete vowed revenge on Blackheart Eddie."

"What happened?" Howie asked.

Ranger Lily stared at the full moon for a moment before answering. "Coyote Pete challenged Blackheart Eddie to a duel. They were to meet at the corral under a full moon. Blackheart Eddie agreed, but it was just another of his tricks.

"Pete searched the corral for Blackheart Eddie. Of course, Eddie wasn't there. He never planned to show up. Coyote Pete was making his way around the herd of horses when his luck ran out for good."

"What happened?" Carey blurted out.

"A coyote broke out in a long howling song," Ranger Lily continued.

"That doesn't sound unlucky," Liza said. "Coyote Pete liked the sound of coyotes."

Ranger Lily nodded. "Coyote Pete liked their howls, but those horses in the corral didn't. The coyote's song spooked the herd and they stampeded. Coyote Pete was caught right in the middle of it."

"That's terrible," Melody said.

"It was," Ranger Lily told the group of third-graders. "Some say Pete's ghost still roams these hills. He's roping wild horses trying to keep them from trampling him so he can find Blackheart Eddie and get his revenge."

Just then, a coyote howled from the surrounding hills. Eddie felt a cold shiver go down his spine as he stared into the black shadows of the hills.

7

Ghost Fever

"Do you think we should tell Ranger Lily about the cowboy who said he was Coyote Pete?" Melody asked her friends.

Ranger Lily and Mrs. Jeepers had stayed behind to put out the campfire while the kids made their way to the bunkhouse for the night. Melody pulled her friends to the side of the trail so they could talk.

A full moon shone above, but the hills were blanketed by deep shadows. Wind rustled the leaves, and Liza pulled her shawl closer.

Eddie shook his head and said, "That couldn't have been the real Coyote Pete."

"Eddie's right," Melody said. "If that really was Coyote Pete, he would've been a ghost."

"Well, he did look kind of pale," said Howie, "and he disappeared without a trace."

"That's right," Melody said slowly. "He was gray all over."

Liza gasped. "Do you mean this is a real ghost town being haunted by a real ghost?"

"Of course not," Melody said, patting Liza on the back. "You must've caught a touch of *ghost* fever. After all, there are no such things as ghosts. That old cow-

boy we met this afternoon was just clowning around with us. He's probably sitting in the bunkhouse laughing about it with the rest of the cowpokes right now."

"He didn't look like a clown to me," Howie said.

"He acted serious," Liza said. "Dead serious."

"He definitely looked more like a ghost than a clown," Eddie admitted.

"So you think we saw a real ghost, too?" Liza asked Eddie, her voice trembling.

"No," Eddie snapped. "We saw a fake ghost. Melody's right. The cowboy is in on Ranger Lily's joke and was just fooling with us. That Coyote Pete story is only a fairy tale Ranger Lily made up to scare kids like us."

"It's working, because I'm scared all the way down to my toenails," Liza said.

"Forget the story," Eddie said, "and that old cowboy. We'll probably never see him again. We leave tomorrow, anyway."

"You better hope so," Melody teased Eddie. "Coyote Pete is after someone named Eddie. Blackheart Eddie. You're the only one around here with that name."

"And don't forget," Liza added, "Blackheart Eddie had red hair and freckles just like you."

"Blackheart Eddie sounds just like you," Howie told Eddie.

Melody nodded. "He even liked to play pranks on people, just like you."

Just then the kids heard the thundering of horse's hooves. "It sounds like those are headed our way," Melody said.

"I hope the ghost of Coyote Pete didn't set the wild horses free," Howie said.

"What if Coyote Pete and his ghost horse is coming after us?" Liza whimpered.

Melody looked at Liza. Howie looked at Eddie. Then they all looked toward the corral. A lone figure on a gray horse thundered straight toward them.

"*Run!*" Liza screamed.

Pillow Fight

Liza's heart pounded as she leaned against the inside door of the girls' bunkhouse. "That was too close," Liza said.

"Maybe Coyote Pete didn't see us," Melody said. "After all, it was getting dark."

"Or maybe Coyote Pete really is a ghost and he's still chasing after Blackheart Eddie," Liza whispered seriously. She didn't want the other girls in the bunkhouse to hear. Most of them were getting into their pajamas.

Melody laughed. "Yeah, maybe Blackheart Eddie is one of Eddie's long-lost cousins."

"It's a good thing we leave tomorrow afternoon," Liza said, plopping down on her cot. "The sooner Eddie leaves this place, the safer he'll be. He needs to stay as far away from Coyote Pete as possible!"

"Who cares about ghosts?" Melody said. "How about an old-fashioned pillow fight?" Melody grabbed her pillow and bopped Liza on the head.

Liza giggled, and the two girls sneaked over to Carey. They pounded her with their pillows.

"Stop!" Carey screeched. "You'll mess up my hair!"

The boys weren't having fun in their cabin. In fact, Eddie looked serious when he pulled Howie away from the other boys. "I need to find this Coyote Pete," he told Howie.

"Are you crazy?" Howie asked.

Eddie shook his head. "No, I have to get to the bottom of this mess. I want to find out the truth, the whole truth, and nothing but the truth."

"What if the truth is that Coyote Pete is

a ghost?" Howie asked. "A real ghost and nothing but a ghost?"

Eddie shook his head. "I don't think that's true. I still believe some old coot is playing a trick on us. I bet he's back at his bunkhouse now, laughing his cowboy boots off at scaring us. It makes me mad just thinking about it."

Howie shrugged. "There's nothing we can do about it."

Eddie smiled. "That, my friend, is where you are wrong!"

9

A Howling Good Time

"Come on," Eddie said, grabbing a flashlight from his backpack and heading out the bunkhouse door.

Howie followed Eddie over to the girls' bunkhouse. Eddie tapped on a window. The girls had finished their pillow fight and were on their cots trying to sleep. Liza had just started to dream about riding a white stallion when she heard the tapping. She sat bolt upright in her cot and hissed at Melody, "It's the ghost of Coyote Pete."

Melody gulped, but then listened. "I don't think so," she said. "It sounds like our very own Blackheart Eddie to me." Melody pulled open the door. Sure enough, there stood Howie and Eddie.

The girls stepped outside, and Liza

shook her finger at Eddie. “I almost wet the bed, you scared me so bad!” she said. “I was sure you were the ghost of Coyote Pete.”

Eddie shook his head. “I’m not, but we’re going to find Coyote Pete and bring him to justice.”

“Justice for what?” Melody said.

“For getting me into trouble with the flour mess and for chasing us with a wild horse,” Eddie said.

“You sound like a sheriff talking about justice and all,” Howie said.

“Or the original Blackheart Eddie,” Melody added.

A lone coyote howled in the distance and Liza jumped. “The only thing we need to do is get back in bed where it’s safe,” Liza said.

Melody nodded. “You need to stay as far from Coyote Pete as possible. He *is* after somebody named Eddie.”

“I’m not afraid of Coyote Pete or of a

little howling," Eddie said. "I'm not afraid of anything."

A whole pack of coyotes howled and Melody said, "How about a *lot* of howling?"

Eddie gulped and told his friends, "Howling is not going to stop me. I'm going to find Coyote Pete and I'm going to give him a piece of my mind."

Melody laughed. "Are you sure you have a spare piece?"

Eddie's face turned red. "I'm not going to stand around jabbering anymore. I'm a man of action." He didn't wait to hear another word. Instead, he took off toward the cowboys' bunkhouse.

Liza stamped her foot. "Eddie, you get back here."

Eddie turned around in surprise. Liza didn't usually try to tell anyone what to do.

"You're always getting us into trouble by running off without thinking," Liza said. "You get back here and listen to me. I have an idea."

10

Cowboys in Underwear

"Shhh," Liza said, "don't let Coyote Pete hear you." Liza shined her flashlight on the stack of wood behind the cowboys' bunkhouse. "We can climb up on this wood and peek into that window," she whispered.

"Good idea," Melody whispered. "I'll go first."

"No!" Eddie said. "Let me go!"

"It was my idea," Liza said.

Howie rolled his eyes. "It's big enough for all of us. We'll look together." The four kids climbed up on the woodpile and peeked through the dusty window.

"I can't see anything," Liza whispered. "Move over."

"This window is too dirty," Melody complained. Liza and Melody both shifted to see better. Unfortunately, when they moved, so did the woodpile. Wood rolled in every direction, taking the kids with it. They landed together in a heap.

"OW!" Eddie snapped when he stood up and rubbed his behind.

"This is crazy," Melody said. "We could have really been hurt."

"It was all for nothing," Howie told the girls. "All I saw in there was a bunch of cowboys in their underwear."

Liza motioned the kids away from the cowboys' bunkhouse. "Maybe we have the wrong idea," she said. "According to the legend, Coyote Pete loved coyotes. If he really was haunting Pioneer Frontier, he wouldn't be sleeping in a bunk with a bunch of cowboys. He'd be hiding in these hills."

The four kids looked behind them. Wind shook the tree leaves and a chain rattled on a shed door that was partly hidden by the trees. "Look," Eddie said. "I bet that's the lair of Coyote Pete!"

Before anyone could stop him, Eddie pushed through the undergrowth toward an old shed.

"We have to go with him," Howie said, "and keep him out of trouble."

Liza sighed. "This is what I was trying to avoid. Maybe we should just let Coyote Pete find him."

Melody shook her head. "We need to bring him back before he gets lost."

The three kids hurried after Eddie. Their flashlights cut a weak sliver of light through the black night. They followed the weed-covered path as it twisted up the hill. Vines reached out and snagged their jeans, and Liza was sure she felt a spider tickle her arm as she pushed past a bush.

"Not very many people use this path," Eddie complained.

"It's probably used by only one person, and he's a ghost," Liza whimpered as she brushed at her arms and legs just in case a few more spiders tried to crawl on her.

"This must be the original Coyote Pete's cabin," Eddie said when they finally reached it. The shed looked as old as the trees themselves. The paint had long worn away and boards were nailed over the only two windows. "I bet it's been abandoned ever since Coyote Pete died in that wild horse stampede."

"You're probably right," Liza said. "We might as well go back to our cabins."

"Besides, there aren't any windows to peek into," Melody told her friends.

"Wait!" Eddie said, pointing to an eyeball-sized knothole halfway up one wall, just perfect for spying. Eddie quietly sneaked up to the hole and looked through. "Holy Toledo!" he gasped.

"Let me see," Melody said, pushing Eddie out of the way. Through the knothole Melody saw the flickering flame of a lantern. Ancient-looking cowboy gear filled the tiny space. There were lassos, saddles, whips, boots, and spurs. But the thing that got Melody's attention was a faded note pinned to the wall with a knife. In big letters it said: BLACKHEART EDDIE — WANTED DEAD OR ALIVE — BUT MOSTLY DEAD!

"This really is Coyote Pete's cabin," Liza said with a gulp after all the kids had taken turns looking through the knothole.

"It can't be," Melody said. "The lantern was burning. That means whoever lives in this cabin is still around. A ghost doesn't need a light."

"Maybe this ghost is afraid of the dark," Liza suggested.

Eddie looked at his friends in the moonlight and laughed. Each one of them had a black smudge around their eye where they'd peered into the hole. "You look like raccoons," he teased.

"How can you laugh at a time like this?" Liza whispered. "Your life is in danger."

"Not *my* life," Eddie said. "Blackheart Eddie's."

"Are you sure Coyote Pete knows the difference?" Howie asked.

"I think we should find Ranger Lily," Liza insisted. "We have to tell her the ghost of Coyote Pete is real, and he's planning his revenge!"

11

Stanley

"Do I look like a ghost?" Coyote Pete asked.

All four kids jumped and turned to look at the angry face of Coyote Pete. The moon cast deep shadows on his face. His eyes looked like two black holes in the middle of his skull.

Eddie quickly made up a story. "Liza was just kidding around. She likes to make up stories."

Liza glared at Eddie. She didn't want people to think she told lies.

"What are you kids doing out here in the dead of night?" Coyote Pete asked.

Melody gulped and held a hand over her black eye. Eddie, Liza, and Howie covered their black-rimmed eyes as well. "We were just exploring," Melody fibbed.

Coyote Pete shook an angry fist at the kids. "I don't cotton to lying. Then he glared at Eddie. "It's *you*!" he said, his voice a hiss. "Tell me your name!"

Melody pointed at Eddie. "I'm Melody, and his name is . . ."

Liza slapped a hand over Melody's mouth. "Stanley," Liza said before Melody could utter another word.

Coyote Pete sneered at the kids. "Stanley? That's not who I'm looking for. But if I ever *do* find him, he'll be sorry he heard the name Coyote Pete."

"Let's go," Liza squealed. The kids ran back to their bunkhouses.

Before they went inside, Eddie stopped Liza dead in her tracks. "Why did you tell that cowboy my name was Stanley?" he asked.

"I had to," Liza explained to Eddie, Melody, and Howie. "Whatever we do, we can't call Eddie by his real name. If Coyote Pete hears it, Eddie will be horse manure."

"But did you have to call me Stanley?" Eddie asked. "Couldn't you think of something different?"

"How about if we call you Pig Knuckles for getting us into trouble with Coyote Pete by spying on his bunkhouse?" Melody asked.

"That's not my fault," Eddie said. "That whole spying thing was Liza's idea."

"It doesn't matter," Liza said. "What's important is that Coyote Pete never finds out about you."

"I'm not so sure that we really met the ghost of Coyote Pete," Melody said. "After all, I'm pretty sure ghosts don't ride wild horses."

"But ghosts do get trapped on earth when they have unfinished business," Liza said. "And Coyote Pete has business to finish. He has to get his revenge on Blackheart Eddie. And he never did find his fortune."

"You're right about one thing," Howie said. "If Coyote Pete really is a ghost, he will haunt this town forever unless he settles his unfinished business. But what if there's something better than revenge he needs to finish?"

"What are you talking about?" Eddie asked. "What could be better than revenge?"

"I just might have the answer to your question," Howie told him. "Meet me at the general store first thing in the morning and bring every penny you have. I'll tell you then how we can rid Pioneer Frontier of its resident ghost."

12

Life's Savings

"Cock-a-doodle-doo!" a rooster crowed in the distance.

"I can't believe we're up this early," Eddie grumbled as the kids waited for the general store manager to unlock the door.

"Give me all your money," Howie told his friends.

"Is this a stickup?" Liza asked with a giggle.

Howie shook his head. "Of course not," he said. "It's all part of my plan."

"I'm not handing over my life's savings until you tell me what's going on," Eddie told Howie.

"It's simple," Howie said before explaining his idea.

"Are you crazy?" Melody asked. "That

RAL STORE
SNACK BAR SALOON
CLOSED

will never rid these hills of a ghost crazed by gold fever."

"Besides," Liza said, "you don't know if it will work. I still think Coyote Pete will stop at nothing until he has revenge on Blackheart Eddie." She poked Eddie in the chest just to prove her point.

"You may be right," Howie said. "But there's only one way to find out for sure. Now, hand over your money."

Liza and Melody looked at each other. Then they dug into their pockets and each gave Howie their crumpled green bills. Howie turned to Eddie and held out his hand. Eddie sighed. Then he dug into his pocket and pulled out two quarters and three pennies. "This is it?" Howie asked. "This is your life's savings?"

Eddie shrugged. "There must've been a hole in my pocket," he mumbled.

Howie counted the money and sighed. "I just hope it's enough."

The kids slipped into the general store.

They searched the shelves of pots, pans, ropes, and canned beans. Finally, Howie found exactly what he wanted. After giving the storekeeper all their money, Howie led the way to the path behind the bunkhouse. They followed the trail until they reached the shabby shed in the middle of the woods. "It's up to you," Howie said as he handed Eddie the bag.

"Why me?" Eddie asked.

"Because, Coyote Pete thinks you are the one and only Blackheart Eddie. He needs you to make amends."

Eddie looked each of his friends in the eye. "I'll do it," he said, "but I think it's a waste of time."

Eddie looked around to make sure Coyote Pete was nowhere in sight. Then he hurried to the door of the shed. He pulled a huge package of chocolate wrapped in gold foil out of the bag and placed it in front of the door. It looked exactly like a bag of real gold nuggets. He hoped it was just like the one Black-

CHOCOLATE
COINS

heart Eddie tricked Coyote Pete out of so many years ago.

Suddenly, Eddie shrieked and sprinted back down the trail. Melody, Liza, and Howie raced after him. Eddie didn't stop until they reached the bottom of the hill.

"Why were you running?" Liza panted.

"Because," Eddie said, gulping air, "we weren't alone up there. Someone — or something — was watching us."

Just then, a howl echoed throughout the hills, sending cold chills racing up their necks.

13

The Real Coyote

"Where have you been?" Ranger Lily asked, causing the kids to jump. Ranger Lily stood with her hands on her hips and did not look happy. "Mrs. Jeepers and I have been looking all over for you!"

Liza gulped. Before her friends could stop her, she told Ranger Lily the truth. Liza didn't like to lie. "We've been trying to trick the ghost of Coyote Pete into leaving Pioneer Frontier for good!" she said in a rush.

"Coyote Pete?" Ranger Lily asked. "But that's just a legend."

"No, it isn't. We saw him," Howie said, "and he was after Eddie."

Ranger Lily looked at Eddie. Her eyes grew wide. "Blackheart Eddie was known for his fire-red hair and freckles," she said slowly. "Just like yours."

"What if the legend is true?" Liza asked with a squeal.

"Show me where you saw this ghost," Ranger Lily told the kids. The four kids led Ranger Lily to the old shed.

"This place has been empty ever since I got here," Ranger Lily told them. "You probably just saw a hiker who decided to take shelter here when he was passing through. The story of Coyote Pete is just that. A story. He doesn't really exist. At least, not anymore."

"She's right," Melody said as Ranger Lily turned and headed back toward the settlement. "There are no such things as ghosts."

"Then who took our gold?" Howie asked. The kids looked over their shoulders at the shed. Sure enough, the bag of golden chocolate was gone.

"It can't be," Liza said with a gulp.

Melody shook her head. "You heard

Ranger Lily," she said. "Coyote Pete was just a story. He wasn't real!"

"Coyote Pete may not be real, but Blackheart Eddie is!" Eddie said with a grin as he pulled one golden nugget of chocolate from his pocket.

Before Eddie could pop the candy in his mouth, something rustled through the bushes. The kids turned just in time to see a coyote wink his giant amber eye at them. Then the lone coyote turned and disappeared into the hills forever.

Debbie Dadey and Marcia Thornton Jones have fun writing together. When they both worked at an elementary school in Lexington, Kentucky, Debbie was the school librarian and Marcia was a teacher. During their lunch break in the school cafeteria, they came up with the idea of the Bailey School Kids.

Recently Debbie and her family moved to Aurora, Illinois. Marcia and her husband still live in Kentucky, where she continues to teach. How do these authors still write together? They talk on the phone and use computers and fax machines!

Learn more about Debbie and Marcia on their Web site: www.BaileyKids.com